REINDEER MOON

Written by Mark Kimball Moulton

Illustrated by Deb Strain

This book is dedicated to my wonderful
and cherished family, who have encouraged and
supported my efforts as well as my dreams
over the years. Scott, Arrin, Katie and Taylor...
I love you with all of my heart.

Deb

This story was inspired by and is dedicated to everyone
who keeps the spirit of the season alive year 'round,
most especially my dear friends, Ethel, Cheryl, Leslie,
Cindy and, of course, my beloved Queenie.

Mark

Presented to

_____

on this date

_____

From

_____

Text by Mark Kimball Moulton.
All illustrations © Deb Strain,
licensed by Mosaic Licensing, Inc.
© Copyright 2000
All Rights Reserved. Printed in the U.S.A.

Published by Lang Books
A Division of R.A. Lang Card Company, Ltd.
514 Wells Street • Delafield, WI 53018
262.646.2211 • www.lang.com

10 9 8
ISBN: 0-7412-0816-4

The world is cloaked in beauty,
the fire is burning bright.
The tree is trimmed...the shopping's done,
and all the world seems right.

So, gather all the family 'round,
'cause Santa's coming soon...
and, together, share this magic tale,
this tale of "Reindeer Moon."

A December snow is falling, lightly dusting all the trees,
draping the silent forest in a crystal filigree.

Stepping out onto the back porch, a willow basket in my hand,
I hesitate, in awe of this pure magical dreamland.

I look up to the winter's sky and breathe in the cool, crisp air.
Flakes land upon my lashes and rest gently in my hair.

This has always been tradition, for many, many years,
since we first came to the forest and built this cabin here.

I still remember Grandma, her cheeks all plump and red,
As she carried out her treats at night, making sure her friends were fed.

She said that we were obligated to share the bounty we possessed,
for to live among these creatures, we were very surely blessed.

It was clear to us that there was more that Grandma understood,
about the ways of all her forest friends, and of their lives out in the woods.

She had a certain, gentle way that caused them no alarm.
They knew that she would never let them come to any harm.

With a twinkle in her eye and a smile that lit her face,
She'd hint that there was <u>magic</u> in the forest 'round her place.

"You must be patient, kind and loving if you're to ever see
the magic and the beauty that the forest holds for me."

"Take time to smell the flowers, enjoy the snowflakes as they fall,
and someday soon, you, too, will see the magic of it all!"

We'd gather at the window, with just one candle lit,
And wait 'til her friends stepped forward, approaching bit by bit.

She'd leave carrots for the rabbits and apples for the deer,
then sprinkle cracked corn on the ground in places here and there.

The deer tiptoed in on slender legs, the bunnies softly jumped
to find the treats she'd left for them by the old pine tree stump.

Often squirrels would join them, or perhaps some playful mice.
We even had a regal moose indulge us once or twice.

I have many good, fond memories of our cabin in the woods,
but one stands out from all the rest, as I'm sure you'll see, it should!

Now, this tale that I'm about to tell is truly a delight,
about a very special reindeer that came to us one night.

Grandma had just finished her nightly feeding chores,
and was shaking off the snowflakes as she entered the back door.

We were curled up near the window, all cozy, safe and warm,
waiting for our forest friends to visit in the storm.

The air was cold and brittle, the ground fresh topped with snow,
when in the deep, dark forest, there appeared the faintest glow.

It might have been reflection, we couldn't really tell...
perhaps moonlight on a patch of ice, or on a tree that fell.

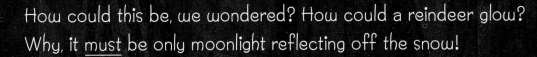

We saw the slightest movement, then the suggestion of an ear,
and suddenly we realized, what was glowing was a deer!

How could this be, we wondered? How could a reindeer glow?
Why, it <u>must</u> be only moonlight reflecting off the snow!

And then, while we were watching, fascinated by the sight,
the reindeer turned as if to go, to vanish in the night.

But as he turned, he stumbled and fell in the fresh, new snow.
He dropped his head and closed his eyes and began to lose his glow!

"Why, he must be hurt or starving!" Grandma cried and donned her cloak.
"We must hurry now and help our friend. Don't dawdle! Let's not poke!"

We grabbed our coats and mittens and followed Grandma out the door,
the air so cold and biting, it chilled us to the core!

Cautiously we touched the deer that lay there in the snow,
and much to our surprise we found it <u>was</u> the deer that glowed!

And not just from falling moonlight, reflecting off his fur,
but from some other inner place, this warm, soft glow occurred.

There was no time then to wonder. We had to get him warm.
Grandma said, "Let's bring him in, out of this winter storm!"

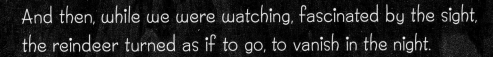

So we wrestled and we struggled
to get the deer inside.
But we could barely budge him,
no matter how we tried.

'Twas then his lashes flickered,
he opened just one eye.
It was big and brown and beautiful—
intelligent, yet shy.

He looked at us as if to say,
"I'll give it one more try,"
and magically, he seemed to float,
he almost seemed to fly!

We wrapped our arms around him
and guided him inside.
We brought him to the crackling fire
and laid him right beside.

Grandma wrapped him in a blanket,
then urged us, "Let him be.
Food and warmth and a good long rest
is surely what he needs."

She placed a wooden bowl beside him,
filled with apples, grain and corn.
He ate a bit, then closed his eyes and soon began to snore!

And though this is most unusual, I must insist that it is so—
with each and every breath he took, his fur would faintly glow!

Once in awhile he snorted, a deep, rich, satisfying sound,
or shifted on the blanket as he would turn around.

But mostly he just lay there, and soon we grew quite tired,
from all the day's excitement, and from the warm and cozy fire.

Grandma ushered us to bed,
up the old and creaky stairs.
She covered us with thick down quilts
and helped us say our prayers.

And though we tried to stay awake
as we lay there in our beds,
visions of sweet, sugared treats
soon danced within our heads.

Much later, around midnight,
something woke me from my dreams.
Nothing I could recognize,
more like a feeling, it would seem.

I rubbed the sleep out of my eyes
and sat up in my bed.
The room was bathed in radiance
from the full moon overhead.

As I peered out of the window
of my tiny upstairs room,
I saw our friend, the reindeer,
fly straight across the moon!

I threw my eyes wide open and ran to wake the rest,
but by then our friend had vanished. "It was just a dream,"
they did suggest. I crept downstairs to see if he
was still asleep down there. But sure enough, he'd left us.
Our deer had disappeared!

The coals still burned upon the hearth,
casting shadows 'cross the room.
I sat in the dark, bewildered...
did he actually
fly across the moon?

The next day it was Christmas Eve. There was so much left to do!
We had to find the perfect tree and wrap the presents, too.

There was barely time to wonder if our reindeer was alright,
or if he would ever come again and visit us some night.

Although quietly I questioned
if I was crazy as a loon,
for I really thought I saw that deer
fly straight across
the moon!

Grandma roasted chestnuts and cooked a fine, fat goose.
The rest of us searched the woods and found a ten-foot spruce.

We strung popcorn and cranberries and draped them on the tree,
while Grandma sat and watched us with a cup of Christmas tea.

The air was sweet with cinnamon, roast goose and fresh pine boughs.
Warm cider bubbled on the hearth. Peace settled on our house.

Our eyes were growing weary and when the clock began to chime,
we yawned and stretched and realized it was almost our bedtime.

We kissed Grandma and said goodnight. She smiled and gave a wink.
"Aren't you forgetting something? A most important chore, I think?"

"After all, it's Christmas Eve. Let's prepare a special treat -
a gift for all our forest friends,
something good for them to eat."

So Grandma packed her basket
with fresh goodies from her store –
carrots, nuts and apples, popped corn and so much more.

We searched along the forest's edge for the perfect evergreen,
and found the cutest, pint-sized tree that you have ever seen!
We placed apples on its branches, arranged carrots 'round the base.
The garland of fresh popped corn hung like delicate, fine lace.
Raisins, nuts and corn completed the effect.
When we were done, we all agreed...our gift was just perfect!

We slept safe and sound that Christmas Eve,
dreaming of the morn,
when we would wake and celebrate
the day Jesus was born.

When the forest birds began to sing
and the mantle clock chimed eight,
we woke and we were all surprised
that we had slept so late!

We jumped out of bed, dressed quickly,
excited and refreshed,
and ran down the stairs to see
what wonders Santa might have left.

We found Grandma
in the kitchen,
cooking eggs and
kneading bread.

"There's something
in the other room for you,"
was all she said.

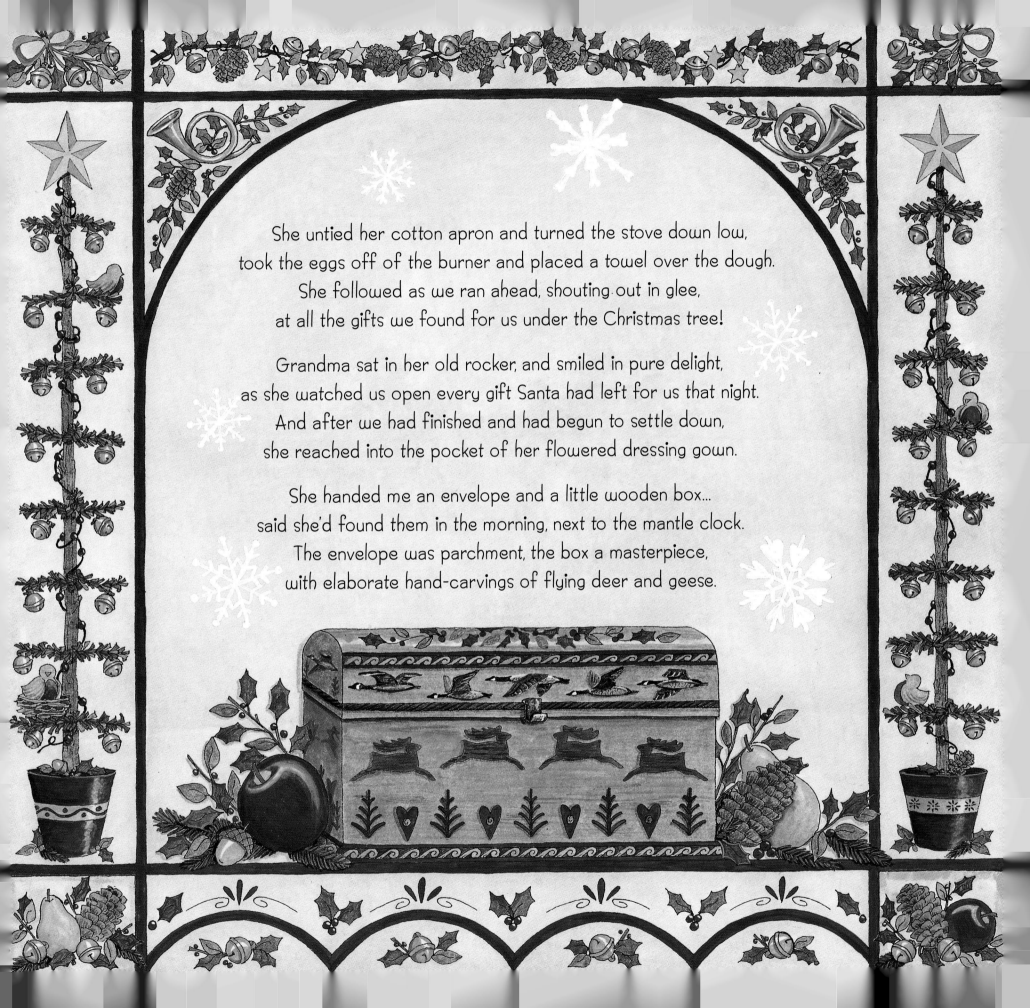

She untied her cotton apron and turned the stove down low,
took the eggs off of the burner and placed a towel over the dough.
She followed as we ran ahead, shouting out in glee,
at all the gifts we found for us under the Christmas tree!

Grandma sat in her old rocker, and smiled in pure delight,
as she watched us open every gift Santa had left for us that night.
And after we had finished and had begun to settle down,
she reached into the pocket of her flowered dressing gown.

She handed me an envelope and a little wooden box...
said she'd found them in the morning, next to the mantle clock.
The envelope was parchment, the box a masterpiece,
with elaborate hand-carvings of flying deer and geese.

She encouraged me to
open up the letter carefully,
for the paper looked quite fragile
and very old indeed!

The script was truly beautiful,
with bold and fluid strokes—
flourishes and curlicues,
most classically baroque!

I first looked at the signature
and could not believe my eyes,
for the letter was from Santa Claus
to all of our surprise!

Everyone cried out for me
to read them Santa's note,
so I sat down by the fireplace
and started, and I quote:

My Dear Friends,

For many years, I've been aware of all your thoughtful ways, caring for our forest friends with tenderness and grace. Your loving home has always been a safe port in a storm...so peaceful, kind and happy...so comforting and warm.

I doubt you are aware of all the goodness that you do, but your kind ways saved Christmas for the world this year, it's true!

The other night, as we were placing stars among the trees, (that we use as flight directionals every Christmas Eve), a blizzard fell upon us, the likes you've never seen. Snow battered us in seconds, the wind blew and howled and screamed!

In all of the confusion my reindeer, Donder, lost his way—wandered 'round for hours, hungry and tired, I'd say. 'Twas then he stumbled here, upon your cabin in the wood, where he found food and shelter, and you treated him so good.

I really don't mind telling you that I was worried sick,
and Mrs. Claus was up all night – she didn't sleep a lick!
Without Donder's help, we knew that my old sleigh would never fly.
We'd <u>never</u> make our trip that night, no matter how we tried.

But, thanks to you, Donder arrived in time to make our flight,
and Christmas is on schedule...all is calm and bright.
But we must hurry now, there's much to do before we see the sun.
So I'll leave this gift with gratitude for all that you have done.

In this special box I've gathered the twinkles from a star
that fell upon a moonlit night from a galaxy, so far.

I stirred in a few warm breezes from a grassy little knoll,
where I sit and watch the sunset near my home at the North Pole.
To this starlight and these breezes, I've added "reindeer glow"...
the magic dust that helps them fly through wind and fog and snow.

When the time has come to make a wish, hold the box,
then close your eyes, and your wish will come true overnight,
before the next sunrise!

Your humble servant, Santa

p.s. No, my friend, you really are not crazy as a loon.
It <u>was</u> Donder that you saw last night fly straight across the moon!

Needless to say, that Christmas
was a joyful, happy day!
We felt proud that we had helped
Donder and Santa out that way.

Every Christmas after that,
we'd watch from our bedrooms,
hoping to see him, once again,
fly straight across the moon.

Everyone was so amazed
that I <u>had</u> seen Donder fly,
and wanted all the details
of how he looked up in the sky.

And though we never saw him,
no matter how we tried,
we knew then, quite for certain,
that some reindeer can fly!

Our forest friends still visit us, each and every night,
when the woods are cloaked in snowfall, and the moon is full and bright.

And the magic of the forest that Grandma had said we'd see,
now brightens every flower, every blade of grass and tree.

For the magic that she spoke about,
right from the very start,
is the love that fills your soul with joy
when you open up your heart!

The hand-carved box
that Santa left was placed into my care.
I never let it out of sight...
I took it everywhere.

For all these years I've treasured it,
this very special box...
wouldn't waste our wish on dolls
or clothes or wooden building blocks.

I wanted the most perfect wish
that there could ever be,
and finally this special wish
has just occurred to me!

Now, I'll close my eyes and make a wish
and hope it does come true...

I wish you all a Merry Christmas

...and a Happy New Year, too!

The End

Other Books to Collect by
Storyteller Mark Kimball Moulton

A Snowman Named Just Bob
Everyday Angels
One Enchanted Evening
Caleb's Lighthouse
The Night at Humpback Bridge
A Cricket's Carol